ANTONIO MELONIO

THE FACTORY
REVOLUTION'S CALL

BOOK 1 OF THE FACTORY SAGA

Copyright © 2023 Antonio Melonio

All rights reserved.

The characters and events portrayed in this book are fictitious. Any similarity to real persons, living or dead, is coincidental and not intended by the author.

ISBN: 9798391768203
Independently published

To the workers of this world.

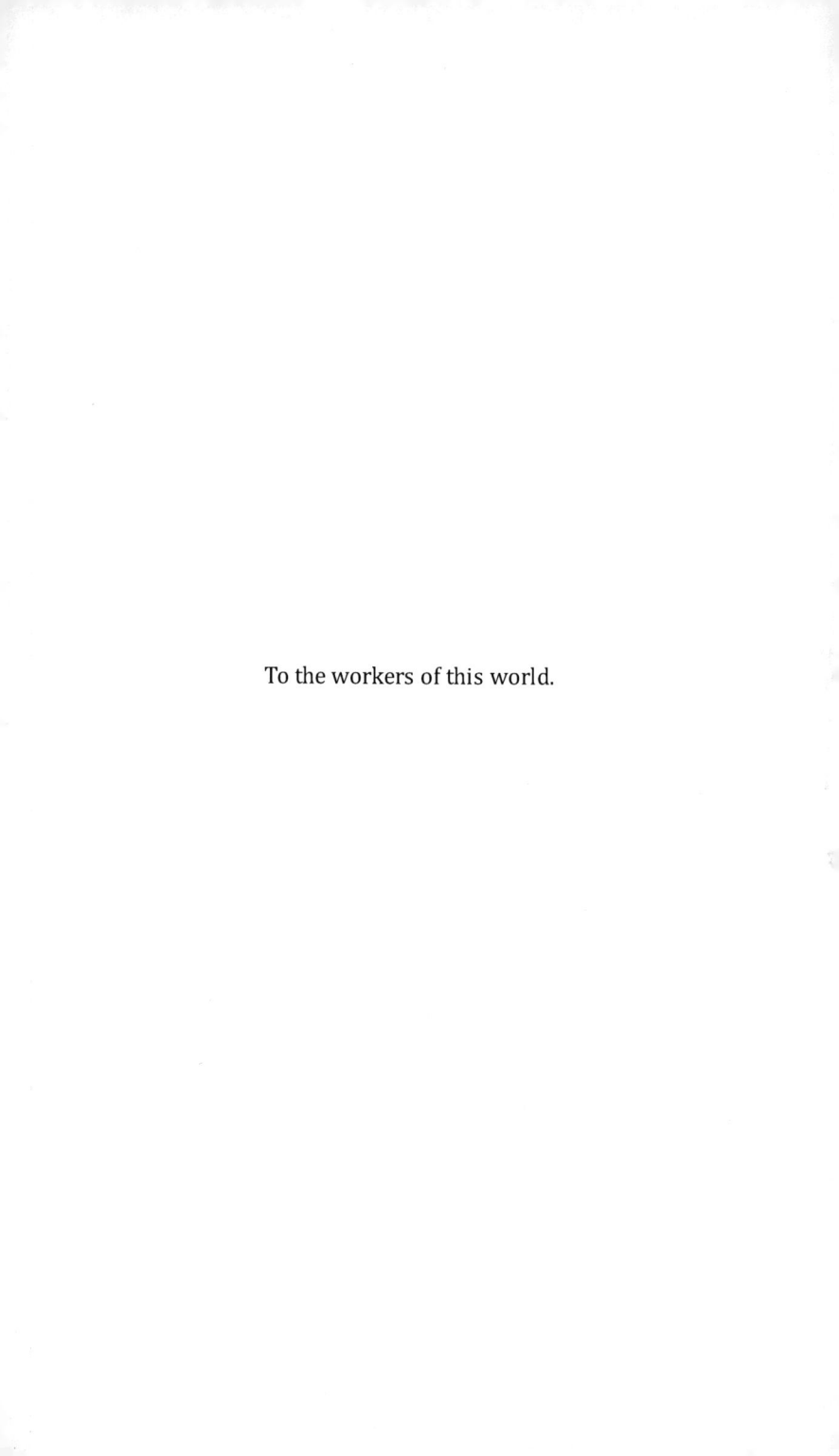

1

I gasped as I opened my eyes to the utter absence of light. Engulfed in an impenetrable blackness with not a sound stirring the lifeless air, my eyes strained to pick out any hint of light. Instead, it was as if I were retreating further into a void, with nothing to anchor me. Floating away in that meaningless space, dissolving and melting. Becoming one with eternity —

With effort, I pulled myself together. My breath grew quicker and shallower as I tried to move and discovered that I couldn't. I was paralyzed. The terror was palpable now, seeping into every corner of my being and leaving me trembling and shaking with fear.

I could feel the cold sweat dripping down my forehead, my heart racing, my body tensing up as I struggled to keep control. I tried to calm myself by inhaling deeply and exhaling slowly, but each breath seemed more futile than the last. My chest burned as if someone had lit a fire in it, and my mind was frantic.

Where was I?

What happened?

I struggled harder against my invisible bonds, but nothing moved. With no light in sight and not a sound to hear, my senses rendered utterly useless, all I was left with was the icy grip of fear that left me trembling in the darkness.

Is this what it feels like to be born?

The oppressive blackness squeezed me tight like an invisible force. An undeterminable, sinister substance that had taken over my entire existence. For a few moments, I almost welcomed it, hoping it would swallow me and end this torment.

I looked around. I could not discern any kind of shape or geometry — not even a trace of it. The only thing that gave meaning to this world, the only thing that confirmed to me that, yes, I was still alive in some grotesque way, were my body's useless exertions. It was the only thing to permeate the stillness of this lonely universe I found myself in.

Minutes passed, maybe hours; it could have been days or weeks for all I know. Still, I fought the darkness.

I tried to remember how I had ended up here, grasping for any shred of memory from before this endless void. But no matter how hard I tried, my mind remained stubbornly blank. Time seemed to have stopped altogether; a slithering fog, with tendrils made of clay and cotton, slippery and intangible. Seconds, minutes, hours; it was all the same to me. I was trapped, suspended here, with neither a way to escape nor mark the passage of time.

And then, without warning, a feeble spark of light from above. Flickering into existence, winking from the darkness. It appeared an infinitely long distance away, soothing and warm, but so very frail it was almost impossible to make out. I felt its presence on my skin like a cloud of close particles, smashing violently into each other, each collision yielding more of the precious warmth. It was not much, this light, but enough to awaken me from my primal onslaught. Bit by bit, I observed as the world around me emerged from absolute blackness. And I with it.

I looked down and saw my silhouette now. My weak body enveloped in filthy, colorless rags I had never seen before, sitting on some kind of iron chair, bound in thick chains as imposing and absolute as the void itself. As I struggled against them, I could feel the cold metal biting into my skin. Six times they encircled my torso, wrapping tightly around my arms. Yet despite their relentless grip, they were wound loose enough to allow my body's heavy breaths to escape.

Sweat beaded on my forehead as I fought against the chains, over and over, desperation fueling my strength. They would not yield.

The chair I was pressed upon, I saw now, was fixed and unmovable, its heavy iron legs molded into the grey concrete floor. Despite that, invigorated by the warmth from above, I tried to shift my weight in a foolish attempt to topple the chair, pushing against the chains that cut into my arms and torso. I tried again and again, but to no avail.

The tides of panic returned as I realized that the light had given me false hope. With each attempt to move, I was reminded of my plight and the bleakness of the situation. *There was nothing I could do.*

I felt myself slipping, my breaths unable to keep up, the numbness taking over until I was nothing but a helpless vessel, swaying in oblivion.

How long I slept then I cannot, with any confidence, tell. There seemed to be no progression in this world. No development, no evolution, no complexity, no dynamic, no life, no indication of time passing, of cause and effect. The darkness, weakly illuminated by the faint light above, appeared an unmoving natural constant and I destined to be the sole witness to its existence.

The failure to remember anything from before made me realize that the darkness had, in fact, always been there. Unnoticed, yet eternal. It signified the end of the circle, the end of the struggle, the goal reached and cherished. There was to be no development past this point. This is it. *This is what we made.* There could not be better, for that would mean that darkness could be improved upon. *Sacrilege!*

In this place I found myself, there was no day. No sun coming up to warm me in its light. There was no movement of air, no smells; even the temperature seemed undeterminable. I felt only the heavy chains upon my body and the suffocating black upon my heart.

Madness became the status quo.

In uncontrollable bursts, like waves crashing on the shores of some distant beach, uncovered beneath a layer of pavement, the panic broke out over and over again. The tides of my existence.

From time to time, and seemingly from very far away, I heard myself screaming.

2

I jolted from a dreamless sleep, still trying to come to my senses, when I noticed that I could now, with much higher clarity, discern the shapes of my body and the chair it was forced upon. I looked up and saw that the faint light from above had become much brighter, blinding my eyes and filling the space with luminous streams. Dust particles were dancing in them like fairies from some faraway land of fantasy.

As my eyes slowly adjusted to this new reality and my mind began comprehending the insanity, I discerned in the distance so very diffuse, so very impossible, and yet more real than anything else in this place, something entirely terrible: in every direction I turned I saw people sitting on chairs.

They were chairs of iron, just like mine.

Rows upon rows of grim figures in the same filthy robes. Thousands of them, uncountable. Chained to their chairs, molded into the ground in an endless dark space, all facing in the same direction. Some seemed unconscious or asleep, some were glancing around in desperation.

I could sometimes discern their eyes, reflecting the weak light from above and shimmering in the blackness like colorful prisms. I wanted to help and comfort these people — my people; they were just like me. Prisoners of this place. I wanted to free them. To shout at them to do something. To rise and break their chains. But I could not bring myself to do it, for I could not even help myself.

And then I heard it. A low, rumbling sound. Soft at first, but growing louder and more powerful by the moment. It seemed to originate from the same distant light above, and slowly, the entire space around us began to quiver and palpitate.

The ground beneath us trembled, the surrounding air vibrated, and the people on the chairs of iron rose mechanically, one by one, their heavy chains falling to the ground like snakes eager to get away from their prey. As if they had been waiting and anticipating this moment.

I could now make out the other prisoners' faces, and my heart sank at the sight of them: pale, malnourished, and frail memories of people. Some of their eyes glazed over to me with exhaustion and despair.

This is not birth; this is hell.

I was one of them now. I had to be, for my chains had fallen off too. The last one to remain seated, I too finally stood and joined the endless rows of the desperate, eager to be a part of this horrible circus. Afraid of being left behind, of being alone in the darkness. We stood there as one, in this infinite dark space, to whence silence once again returned.

I remember feeling a distant echo of power in this moment. Here we were, the desolate and the miserable. Each of us entirely insignificant on our own. Just a mass of feeble weak minds, slaved to vehicles of flesh, clothed in rags, and bound in chains both visible and imagined. But together, we were something more. Put us over the edge, push us too far, and we would tear you apart. For the first time, I felt something approaching strength — fragile as it was.

The moment passed as the deep rumbling sound returned and shook the earth once more. Terror and helplessness, once again, took over the reins.

From behind us, like an approaching storm front, an army of tall bulky figures in grey uniforms appeared. They moved, their footsteps like thunder shaking the ground until they were surrounding us; were between us. I watched in terror until they finally stopped, facing in the same direction as we did.

I saw that their dark uniforms were tight and crisp, their tall, black boots polished to a glossy, mirror-like sheen. The soldiers — for what else would they be? — were tall and strong, a youthful zeal in their eyes. Each had a rifle — metal beasts, forged and molded to perfection. Their black finishes shimmered in the light like mirrors. They were long and elegant, sculpted pieces of machinery. I couldn't take my eyes off them.

Now, the soldiers were close enough to see their faces, yet they stood as if they were not really present. Impassive and brutal. As if they were not human, but mindless machines of destruction. And I wondered if they did not share the same agonies as we did. The same heartaches and longings, the same trials and joys. Were we not their brothers and sisters? Were we not the same?

The sound stopped and after a moment of silence we started moving forward in unison, step by step, led by the soldiers. I had no choice but to comply. It was something I did not have to be told. Something apparent, like second nature. It was either comply or die right there. I knew that without being told.

And then I took the next step and the one after that.

The soldiers kept their eyes facing to the front, not a twitch on their faces, not a trace of compassion in them. They never even looked at us. Like automatons, they walked on and on. But where were they leading us?

We continued walking towards an unknown destination, prisoners and guards marching in silence until, after what felt like an eternity, a dim, long-stretched shape began to appear in front of us. As we got closer, I could make out a tall impenetrable gate made of iron and steel. A hot, bitter wind carrying the smells of oils, molded metal, and otherworldly chemicals wrapped around me as a call resounded from beyond the monstrosity. It was a cruel voice of stone and sand, of fire and iron, of time and emptiness.

"Welcome to the Factory," it boomed.

The gate screeched open, the rusty hinges groaning in protest. An artificial and weak crimson hue illuminated the area and cast an eerie shadow over us. Eyes peering out from beneath uniformed caps pointed forwards, and we could do nothing but obey and trudge ahead.

With each step, the light revealed more details of the sinister facility, so massive it could barely fit into our minds. My heart raced as I tried to make sense of what I saw. The high walls to the sides of the gate stretched endlessly in all directions, an abomination of concrete and bricks. Inside, below gloomy red neon lights and tall smokestacks, workers in rags stumbled back and forth, their faces full of pain. Everywhere I looked and turned, I saw endless rows of production lines, conveyor belts, warehouses, crates, and barrels, while the sound of machines and strange smells filled the stagnant, murky poison air.

And above it all, stretching into the pitch-black sky, was

a giant tower rising from the factory floor, its peak reaching for the heavens. Shiny white marble surfaces, gem-adorned ornaments, and a golden crown that formed the top of its colossal spire reflected the cold dark lights of the Factory. The omnipresent smoke extended and contorted their dimensions. The Tower seemed to me a beacon of hope and oppression at the same time, and I wondered what it was for and who or what lived there.

As we continued forwards, the figures in grey uniforms leading us, the suffocating atmosphere of the Factory swallowed me up. I could feel a darkness descend over my soul; a darkness that, I knew, would never again leave me. I was a prisoner of this place — we all were — and I knew we could never escape. This was my reality now, the reality of all of us.

And this was the world of the Factory.

3

We were received by twisted humanoid silhouettes in black suits and thin red ties. They seemed almost alien, their facial features distorted and blurred, illuminated only by the cold red neon. The shadows of their elongated slender forms stretched and quivered along the machines, walls, and floors as they walked the dark alleys of the Factory. They appeared emotionless and yet graceful, staring into illuminated receptacles as they carried out their tasks of monitoring and directing. In deep distorted voices, they divided us into groups and put us to work.

We moved in a robotic trance, following the suits' orders without thinking. The tasks they gave us were mundane and repetitive, but we knew if we didn't do them, they would break us — always, the grey soldiers patrolled within shouting distance. We toiled in silence and sweat, the machines and contraptions running around us like the ticking of a timer.

It was all a blur — the noise of the machines, the somber red lights, the oppressive heat, the choking smoke, the smell of oil and chemicals, and blood and sweat. Everywhere, the same scenes repeated in an endless loop.

We were tiny cogs in a great machine that consumed

unintelligible raw materials and churned out products we never saw. A never-ending cycle of work and exhaustion. I watched as some of us were broken down, our spirit and sanity slipping away with each passing moment.

The grim red, the smog, the smokestacks, the machines, the contraptions and the mechanisms, the conveyor belts, the workers, the piles of corpses, the production lines, the grey soldiers, the deafening noise, the rats, the slender suits and their long shadows, the glimmering tower reaching for the heavens, limbs caught in cogs, spilling incandescent blood. Work, work, work, unending toil. Do or fucking die!

We were allowed no rest, working on the same ever-repeating utterly useless tasks, with no goal in sight, no end to the toiling and the sweating, no reward but more work. Exhaustion became just as much a natural constant as the Factory itself.

Time had no meaning in this place. The Factory had always been there; there was nothing else — there could not be, and we would remain here forever.

As I lifted my hammer again and again and again, I realized with a sudden clarity that — besides the utter blackness of my birth — this oppressive dark place was the only world I have ever known. We were indeed the forgotten — we, the laborers of the Factory. We kept working, and we kept enduring, and we kept hoping that one day something would change. But until then, we were nothing but tortured spirits, lost in a place that was never supposed to exist in the first place.

We were not fed, for we were beyond hungry; we did not sleep, for the machines never did; we did not talk, for talk was forbidden; we did not complain, for complaining meant certain death. There was only one reality, one need, one desire — the hunger of the machine. Churning out resources and bodies to help fuel the beast that was the Factory.

The Tower kept on growing.

And so we worked. And we died. Others came. A never-ending inpour of workers. There were never shortages or outages. The cycle kept going as if nothing had ever existed other than the Factory, as if the world had never known anything else. We were prisoners to this pulse; this rhythm of production and progress.

This is our tale, and it's a grim, dark one no one will ever want to hear. We will never be remembered or have our suffering acknowledged. Ours was a world of darkness, a world of lies and oppression, and no one would ever save us. We were souls lost in a forgotten place, waiting and hoping for a miracle. And all the while, we kept on working without complaint, our hammers and wrenches tightening those devilish contraptions as our bodies were slowly broken down.

4

Despite the perpetual darkness of the Factory, we learned to mark the passage of time by the subtle patterns of activity we observed. So when a group of slender suits appeared from around the corner, talking to each other in their deep, distorted voices, we knew that another unspecified period had passed.

As we labored, carrying perfectly uniform reddish-brown bricks from the conveyor belts of one machine straight to the mouths of another that immediately consumed and turned them into red dust, the suits approached, their gracious footsteps echoing through the facility.

We heard them discuss how the brick-producing machine could be further improved. How to increase its efficiency; how to produce more while putting in less. We watched as they discussed the intricacies of the apparatus and its various components, their long fingers manipulating geometric shapes on their bright rectangles.

They were also talking about us, their servants, and how they could make us work harder and faster. Their narrow mouths moved, producing warped imitations of sounds we could barely understand, while the rest of their faces twitched in incomprehensible patterns. We were nothing more than a means to an end in their eyes. Tools to be used and discarded at will. We listened with a mixture of dread and blind anger.

The machines were constantly changed and improved. The suits and their shiny rectangles appeared everywhere, analyzing, directing, analyzing again, increasing output, reducing input, maximizing labor. We were never told, but we understood all the same: the Tower and the Factory itself had to grow or they would die. Stagnation could not be allowed; everything had to be improved all the time. Constant growth was not just an outcome or by-product; it was the goal itself. Producing and consuming in endless, self-sustained, senseless loops. Most of the enormous machines seemed to serve no practical purpose, but existed merely for the sake of existing — and all of them demanded a myriad of workers.

Despite the growing challenges and harsh conditions, we persisted. Our muscles strained and our backs ached as we lifted heavy tools and machinery, our feet pounding the conveyor belts and scarcely illuminated alleys as we stretched ourselves thin and raced to keep up with the relentless pace of the machines. We toiled tirelessly, tightening bolts, welding frames, and hammering away as sparks flew around us and smoke choked our lungs. Slender suits and grey soldiers watched our every move.

And as we worked, we noticed that the gleaming tower was growing taller and taller, as if by unseen forces. No workers were allowed there, yet still its base became broader and its spire larger.

The façade shone with more gems than before; the golden crown grew more intricate and imposing, while the rest of the Factory rotted away in dirt and darkness. The stench of

The Factory

chemicals and decay that permeated everything was not so strong near the Tower. There was no smoke there. Sometimes, one could even smell subtle spices and wood, and some kind of food. In the area around the Tower, however, more and more rats appeared, eating away at the scraps and the piles of bodies that speckled the landscape of the alleys between the machines. From the very beginning, we were made certain of what waited at the close of our mortal existence.

On and on the Tower grew.

5

As the three of us fed an undeterminable yellow liquid that burned our noses and stung our eyes into painted-red barrels of aluminum, one of the laborers to our side, a thin woman with short pale hair, collapsed to the ground.

We could hear her piercing cry through the red twilight as she dropped, the barrel she had attempted to lift and carry still cradled in her arms. Droplets of sweat covered her forehead as tears rolled down her cheeks. The veins stood out on her neck and she was panting. She had reached her limit and knew this was the end. Soon she would join the rotting piles of bodies scattered throughout the Factory, nourishing the rats.

We rushed to her side as she lay on the ground, lifted the heavy barrel aside, and tried to raise her. We knew we had only seconds to save this woman from certain death.

Just then, three of the Factory's soldiers appeared, rifles raised and aimed. Ready to deal death as if it was nothing. We stood still like statues, unable to move or breathe.

The woman in our midst hugged us closer, gripping our shoulders, her face betraying her terror. The soldiers' faces were hard and set and they had no intention of mercy. I was rooted to the spot and time seemed to pass without movement; apparently, my heart had stopped beating. The entire factory went silent for a moment.

And then, just before they could fire, another soldier appeared from behind one of the vast machines.

Towering over us with broad shoulders, the newcomer's bald head gleamed in the dim red light of the Factory. His muscular, sweat-slicked body exuded strength as he stood before us, his dark skin seeming to absorb the flickering twilight. There were badges on his uniform and I could see a black tattoo on the lower end of his right forearm, appearing and disappearing beneath his uniform as he moved closer. I couldn't quite make out its shape, but it looked like a hammer.

The newcomer barked an order, gesturing for the others to lower their weapons and stand down. After a few long moments of uncertainty, the soldiers complied, setting their rifles aside and glancing at one another in confusion. A wave of silent, almost unimaginable hope washed over us as the tension momentarily dissipated.

Although we could not quite understand his words, we could feel the commanding presence of the newcomer as he kept bellowing and raging, his voice a resonant, guttural roar. We watched in uncertainty as the other soldiers, their faces hard as granite, finally turned and trudged away, fading into the shadows. Still, we stood like statues, unable to move and think, the woman between us sobbing and clinging to our shoulders.

The soldier with the tattoo turned to us with eyes full of sorrow and conflict. He appeared to be looking for something — something he hadn't found in the other soldiers. Something that went beyond words. In a hesitant, almost unintelligible whisper that stood in stark contrast to his imposing stature, he uttered two words so improbable that it took us a few moments to realize what they meant.

"Help her," he whispered, his eyes wavering and his hands shaking.

He seemed ready to collapse right there, right in that moment. Ready to embrace us, his comrades, and be among equals. Leave behind his own shackles and chains. Break the invisible barriers that held us apart — two sides of the same abused coin — and begin living.

Alas, he could not.

I saw him glance at the Tower. It could be seen from all corners of the Factory, no matter how far away one stood. Always present, watching, luring, and pacifying. It seemed to promise so much. Would one be allowed to enter if one worked hard enough? Upon death, perhaps? Oh, to live among the marble, the gems, and the gold. To find food, warmth, and comfort. To find an end to the pain, the salvation promised.

Or to burn it all down.

I saw these thoughts racing through his mind as if they were my own. Saw his struggle and inner turmoil, for it was mine too. Momentarily, our eyes met and understanding was exchanged. Are we not the same? So many of us, but only one tower. We could not possibly all fit in there.

We broke our paralysis, and my comrades and I turned to the woman still sobbing in our midst, comforting her with silent gestures. I glanced to where the soldier had been standing just a moment before and saw that he was gone.

We led the woman to a safe place, a sort of depression between two machines, where the soldiers would not find her so easily. There, she would be granted a brief rest, and then she would return to work. As we turned to leave — to return to our own tasks before we were discovered — I caught a glimpse of her face and saw that it was contorted now, not with fear, but with rage.

6

The soldier's two simple words echoed in our minds as we returned to our tasks, our eyes watering from the acid we handled. His words were like beacons of light in the darkness; they reminded us that even amidst all our suffering, we could still choose kindness and compassion over cruelty and destruction.

We could not speak, for every word summoned the suits and consequently the soldiers. Still, the tale of the soldier with the tattoo of a black hammer spread like wildfire through the Factory. Told in glances and gestures. In smiles and fleeting emotions.

We kept on toiling, but now we felt a sense of purpose in our labor. We kept on suffering, but our lives appeared now in a different light. A new perspective had opened up. The Tower did not appear so alluring anymore. More and more, we came to think of it as an obstacle. As something that stood between us and the indescribable things, we didn't even know we were longing for. It burned in our hearts, as well as in our eyes.

Amidst all the horrors, we now found hope in each other as strangers became comrades, as eyes met across factory floors with understanding glistening within them. We held onto those moments for dear life, for it was all we had to fight against this relentless prison. We had no language to speak with each other, no touches to exchange, and little strength to resist the machines, but something inside us kept us going, kept driving us forward.

There was a deep solace to be found within each other, we discovered. Within shared suffering, collective pain, and mutual hope. A kind of solidarity no one besides us could ever understand.

We were not dead yet.

We were alive!

Another hour, another day, another year, another eternity.

Not dead yet, just not yet.

We found comfort in the shedding of secret tears; in whispered sounds, not quite words, but even so incredibly powerful. We found ambition in work done poorly — in small, undiscoverable acts of sabotage to slow down the gears of the machine. And always we thought of the soldier and what had become of him.

His black hammer became our symbol, his words became our credo.

"Help her!" our hearts screamed.

7

The change in our demeanor did not go unnoticed.

An army of suits, walking in perfect rows, their delicate and long bodies swinging back and forth, came striding from the Tower's entrance to inspect the Factory, pushing their way through the workers to ask questions. They knew the entire story, knew what had happened, yet they could not find the soldier with the black tattoo — and they could not identify the workers that had borne witness to it all. We all looked the same to them, with our colorless rags and oily abused faces.

Many of us they interrogated, and some they dragged to the dungeon-like depths of the Tower, where soldiers forced them to their knees. The darkness echoed with their screams as tales told of an eyeless suit with dark dripping holes in his face. It moved about them, they said, raking the long cruel fingers of its curved arms across the most exposed parts of their bodies, searching for weaknesses, cutting and probing and sawing with instruments of gold. Others spoke of a soldier with an imperfect mask, aiding the suits with traces of... life in him. All just tales, I thought.

Yet sometimes, when we worked close to the Tower, we would hear echoing cries and shrieks. Then, our bodies would shake, and we'd work with terror and sorrow in our hearts. Barely able to lift our tools, our imaginations running wild but never quite approaching the horrors of reality. More than a few of us lost their minds listening to this agony, and working near the Tower became its own sort of torture.

When those who returned from the depths emerged, their bodies were scarred and mutilated. Some were missing limbs, others blinded by the horrors they had witnessed. Many bore bloody wounds where their noses used to be, their minds scarred forever by the insanity of what they had seen. Most did not survive long after, their spirits broken and unable to bear the weight of the memories they carried. Some chose to end their suffering and join the piles of corpses, unable to face the prospect of living with what they had endured.

Yet no matter how many times they asked the same questions, no matter how many of us they tortured and for how long, still they had no answers. No one could tell them anything. No one knew who the soldier was, what he looked like, or where he had gone. And no one knew who the workers were that had witnessed it all.

I had been lucky. I did not have to experience the physical torment myself, for I likely would have broken and told them of the tattoo. The other workers did not know why the black hammer had become our symbol and I would not tell them even if I could. Still, the pain of my comrades became my pain — our shared agony. Every injury they inflicted upon one of us became an injury to us all. Every slight, every hardship, every injustice, every new form of misery they came up with. *Everything*. And we would remember it all.

The suits, once so confident and intimidating, seemed now to almost slink away from us, always walking in large groups, escorted by grey soldiers. They seemed aware of the new power we carried. They could do to us whatever they desired and still they could not extinguish the spark. Once it was there, it remained, and the Factory changed forever. We could feel their unease as if *they* were now the ones in chains. It made them angry — and unpredictable. I remember smiling, once.

8

More soldiers came. Different ones.

They arrived in formidable formations, walking in a procession from the gates, whence we all came from, to the Tower. Their heavy boots marched in unison, scattering the rats that fled between our naked feet. We watched the unending rows of pitch-black uniforms in silence and fear. When they reached the Tower, they halted, formed huge concentric circles around it, and began to spread out all across the Factory.

These soldiers were far taller — some of them twice the size of our tallest — and carried more powerful weapons. Heavy machine guns with long sinuous barrels and scopes that glinted in the twilight. Round grenades hung from their belts and blinding flashlights cut through the dark alleys.

They began patrolling the narrow pathways between the complex webs of machines, their heavy boots kicking up sparks from the metal floors. The black of the newcomers merged with the grey of the established, forming a tide of terror that washed over the Factory and reached even the most hidden corners and alleys.

They were not like the grey soldiers we knew; the Blackshirts were more callous, cruel, and relentless, with a ferocity that seemed almost animalistic. They targeted workers with specific questions and demands, dragged away anyone who failed to answer, and tortured them until they gave in. So many faces I came to know, so many comrades, disappeared in the dungeons beneath the Tower, only to reappear, after a time, in one of the rotting piles where the rats soon devoured their abused corpses.

Even the grey soldiers, once in charge but now reduced to servitude, were not always safe. Occasionally, we came across cadavers wearing barely recognizable grey uniforms. These bodies were often battered and mutilated beyond recognition, with bruises and injuries covering their skins. It was a gruesome sight that spoke to the brutality and callousness of the Blackshirts, and the complete lack of humanity they displayed toward even those who were on the same side.

We tried to stay strong, but fear spread through the Factory like a plague. Silent rumors of disappearances and mysterious deaths became commonplace, causing panic among even the bravest of us. We had thought ourselves safe as long as we played by their rules, but now we knew that was not true. Every moment, we feared for our lives as the Blackshirts continued their cruel rule, torturing and murdering at will. There were no limits to their savagery and no place where one could feel even a remote sense of safety.

And then, finally, they came for me.

I was working a machine, trying to stay focused despite the constant fatigue and the stinging smoke in my eyes, when I heard the heavy footsteps approaching. I turned, my heart racing, as two towering soldiers in black uniforms stormed up to me.

Without warning, one grabbed me by the arms and the

other choked me with a powerful hand, nearly as large as my torso, preempting any illusion of resistance I might have harbored. Then they began to drag me away from the machine and toward some unknown fate.

There was no resisting these inhuman forces and the only thing I could make out as they forced me along were the eyes of my comrades, following me for as long as they dared. Trying to provide comfort and failing at that, as I recognized the tears and deep sorrow within them.

I was beyond terrified, not knowing what the Blackshirts wanted or what they would do to me. In that moment, I knew that I would break under their torture and tell them whatever they wanted to hear — *everything*. I was not as strong as the others.

Did they know I had witnessed the tattooed soldier's actions? That I had helped spread the story? How could they know? I begged and pleaded with them; I cried, and I sobbed, but it was all for nothing. They did not seem to care. They just sneered at me and dragged me down the dark alleys.

We halted in the vicinity of the Tower. There, the Blackshirts opened a discreet gate guarded by grey soldiers. They escorted me down to the deep dungeons beneath, where they locked me in a cramped, shadowy cell. They secured shackles around my wrists and ankles, and chained me to an iron chair that was bolted to the ground. I could not move even a muscle.

Then they closed the door, and I remembered what it was like to be born.

I remembered the choking, all-encompassing darkness, the loneliness, and the savage panic of these first moments as they returned to me once again. Here I was, back at the beginning of it all. Alone and destitute; my comrades and the yearning for something more brutally taken from me, returned to the dark universe where nothing mattered and everything stayed the same forever. Destined to either vegetate in blackness or toil in the red twilight of the Factory.

What is the purpose of it all? I wondered.

If this is all that can be, then why resist and struggle at all?

Why not just give in — give up?

Will it ever end?

Please, just let it end. I am so very tired.

As time slipped away, twisted, contorted, looped, and stretched, my mind transitioning between unconsciousness and reality, the difference between it all blurring, the only things I remained aware of were my own helpless breathing, the sounds of muffled screams echoing through the dungeon, and the smell of blood and fear in the air.

Then, an eternity passed.

9

I will never know how long they held me in that cell or why they chose to release me. All I know is that when they did, I was nothing more than a shattered remnant of my former self. The time spent in black confinement, subjected to who knows what kinds of treatment, had left me irrevocably changed. I was an empty shell, going through the motions, but no longer feeling truly alive. The person I had once been was gone, and all that remained was a hollow husk, pretending to be me.

From beneath the Tower, a new person emerged. He re-entered the Factory, and he picked up the hammer and the wrench, but it no longer felt the same.

I tried hard, so very hard, to forget about everything and fully immerse myself in the work, but the memories of the never-ending darkness and the constant fear of being returned to it persisted. Every time I closed my eyes, I was back on that iron chair, floating around in the blackness, melting into it. Compared to that, the Factory felt like heaven.

I cherished the pain and the cruelty of the soldiers; I cherished the unending pointless work; I cherished my blemished hands and my broken back, and the blood, and the soothing red neon, and the rats, and the rotting piles, waiting patiently for release. I cherished it all, for anything was better than that cell.

And when I glanced up, I found that the Tower had grown.

It was apparent that my comrades felt a range of emotions toward me. Some looked at me with pity and compassion, perhaps feeling sorry for the suffering I had endured and the state I was in. Others looked at me with disgust, repulsed by the content and acceptance I now felt toward the Factory and our oppressors. All of them, however, saw me as broken, and, in many ways, they were right.

The black void had left me changed, and I no longer felt that I belonged with my comrades. As I looked into their eyes, I saw that they were still fighting! Still defiant in the face of the Tower! And in those moments, I realized that what had happened to me, as terrible as it was, was not important in the grand scheme of things. *It just did not matter.* Not a bit. Compared to the larger struggle, it was nothing.

What mattered was the fight, the collective, and the determination to keep going and not give in. As I looked at them, my comrades, and watched them work, I realized that they were not yet defeated. They had the fire in their eyes, still, and the revolution in their hearts. It was all that mattered.

The spark could not be extinguished unless they killed us all. And they will never do that, for who then would build their golden monuments of vain and their empty fortunes?

I was done; I was destroyed, but these men and women, these comrades of mine, they were not. They would continue and they would not stop. I could never again join them, I felt then — and how foolish I was — but secretly I would long.

10

Time passed; time spent with nothing but work and terror. The Blackshirts were still among us, still haunting the alleys of the Factory, and I tried, slowly, to regain a semblance of my former self.

Then, one time, as we walked through a narrow alley between two colossal machines, the noise deafening and the smoke choking, we stumbled upon a gruesome scene.

The smell of blood and burning flesh joined the chemical vapors and stung our nostrils as my comrade and I scattered into the shadows behind a machine, safely hidden from view. We heard soldiers, both black and grey, rambling to each other, flustered and agitated, the Blackshirts yelling hurried orders. What could possibly excite these cold unfeeling uniforms so much?

My comrade pointed at a narrow gap close to the ground and when I looked through, my body pressed to the cold concrete, I beheld the soldiers scampering around a long humanoid figure that could only be a suit.

The suit moaned in pain, its torso burned and marked with a symbol we could not make out from the distance. Its long limbs, twisted and broken in many places, were tied to four slowly moving metal rods that were connected to a sort of apparatus. Otherworldly shrieks escaped the creature as the apparatus roared and the rods started moving apart.

It all happened in an instant.

First, we heard the ripping of its suit, then the ripping of its limbs, and then the shrieking stopped.

The soldiers froze in their movements and watched with faces of stone as the suit was slowly dying, blood dripping from its remains. No one dared to look away from the gory spectacle. My heart raced, the adrenaline sharpening my senses and making everything seem more real, more vivid than before.

I could not help but feel a pang of sympathy for whatever this creature used to be before it put on the suit. Had it been one of us? A worker trying to survive the relentless wheels of the Factory, ultimately turning against their own kind? Could the same happen to me, if given the chance? Would I take it? I remembered the black cell and wondered if I would rather choose to become a suit than return there. And then I tried not to think of the answer.

As we watched, the Blackshirts started yelling orders again. My comrade and I stayed silent and motionless in the shadows, exchanging nervous glances until finally, the shouting ceased, the air grew still, and the apparatus that had torn the suit's limbs apart stopped its roaring. We waited until the last soldier had left the dark alley, and then came out of our hiding place, holding our breaths.

Reluctantly, we approached the area where the suit's remains were scattered. From our hiding spot, we had only been able to catch glimpses of what had happened, but now, as we stood at the scene, we saw it all and the sight would stay with us forever. Burned in our memories and dreams until the day we died.

The suit's body had been completely disassembled; it was all spread out in myriads of pieces, unrecognizable as ever having belonged to something larger. There was blood everywhere, collecting in pools on the uneven concrete floor. Soon, rats were swarming and drinking them empty, gnawing at the pieces of flesh scattered across the ground. The symbol we had not been able to make out from a distance burned in the partly conjoined suit's chest, shined in the gruesome slurry. Amidst all the blood and gore, I could finally make out what it was.

It was a hammer — but not a black one.

A hammer, red from burned flesh.

11

Exchanged in glances and subtle gestures, the news of the suit's grisly death and the red hammer burned in its chest spread through the Factory. Yet despite the fresh surge of hope and defiance it caused, fears of repercussion and violent punishment became palpable, rising in our throats like bile whenever we saw a soldier pass or heard their boots echoing against the concrete floors.

We all knew that any tiny mistake could cost us our lives now — even more so than before — which is why none of us left even a moment up to chance. Carefully, we worked in an endless flurry, not even daring to look into each other's faces to see what was going on. Out of the corner of my eye, I saw my comrades toiling around me, each absorbed in their tasks, heads held down in a desperate attempt to become invisible and avoid the soldiers' attention. Their voices and heavy footsteps seemed so loud now that our ears were ringing, and they circled us like a pack of starved wolves.

Even I, in my broken state, could not remain indifferent. I thought I had overcome fear and the prospect of death when I had returned from beneath the Tower, but alas, my primal instincts proved me wrong and I cowered away like everyone else, afraid of doing something wrong or drawing attention to myself. Surely, revenge would come. They could not allow such a deed to go unpunished.

The hammers in our hands felt different now. We had crossed a line. One from which there was no coming back. A suit, one of them, one of the untouchables, had died. Murdered in the most gruesome way in the middle of the Factory, among the machines, the rats, and the smoke. The killer had to be one of us. Maybe more of us. What would happen now? We waited for the punishment, dreading the renewed pains it would bring and, at the same time, wishing it would arrive sooner. To have it all over with.

And then it came.

A deep, loud rumbling noise, like that of a vast engine or motor, broke the momentary silence of the Factory.

The sound seemed all too familiar, and I recognized it as the same one that had filled the blackness of my birth when the soldiers had arrived. The memory of that moment, filled with terror and darkness, came rushing back to me as the noise shook the ground beneath our feet and made the machines tremble and shudder. Instinctively, we all stopped dead, dropping our tools and looking up in fear.

I noticed an army of soldiers surrounding us. Blackshirts from one side, soldiers in grey from the other, leaping, shouting orders as they began rounding us up like rats.

I could see the glint of their rifles as they pointed them at us, urging us to move forward. I followed the crowd, trying to stay calm as they pushed and prodded us toward an enormous cleared space between the machines. It was apparent that we were being rounded up for some purpose, but I could not fathom what that might be. All I could think about was the fear coursing through my veins, as I was forced along with the rest of the group.

Thousands upon thousands of us filled that space within minutes, standing there in a semicircle with scarcely enough room to breathe, our hands and feet tightly squeezed together. A packed tangle of bodies writhing and straining. Soldiers separated by uniforms watched from all sides, with many more straight in the front where battalions of Blackshirts stood in formation. They held their weapons ready, scanning the crowd for any signs of disobedience.

Then, one of the grey soldiers fired his rifle in the air and we fell silent and still, holding our breaths. The air was thick with tension as we waited for the Blackshirts to speak or make their next move. Minutes passed in anticipation.

Finally, a man stepped forth from the Blackshirts' formations and sauntered to the middle of the cleared space. He was shorter and slimmer than the others, with dark eyes set deep within his face, and he wore proudly upon his chest an emblem of a white tower. It shone brilliantly beneath the blinding floodlights from above, making him appear more regal and imposing than he was. It was plain that this man held a high rank among the Blackshirts — possibly the highest.

He opened his mouth then to speak, but no words came out at first; instead, he just stared at us, moving from face to face with an almost sympathetic gaze until finally, he broke his silence with three simple words:

"This is justice."

The Blackshirts to our left began marching purposefully, each bearing a twisted armful of splintering timbers to where the man with the emblem — I came to think of him as the General — stood.

The wood looked as hard and impermeable as stone, but the soldiers hacked it apart easily, stacking the pieces in precise patterns on the ground, building up to a large pyre. Their gazes fixed on the General — following his precise instructions — they worked feverishly to assemble the next section: a soaring wooden stake, topped with a scaffold. With each mechanical heave and thrust of their tools, their eyes blazed with determination and purpose, as glimmering droplets of sweat hit the hard concrete floor.

It became quite clear what they were building, and yet, despite our understanding, we remained silent and did nothing. I looked around and realized that there were so many more of us than there were soldiers of either color. We could just swallow them up, if we wanted, machine guns and grenades and all. And still, we seemed frozen in place, too weak, too pathetic to take action. I couldn't help but wonder why my comrades and I were so paralyzed, why we were just standing there waiting for the horrible play to resume. They had hoarded us here like rats, and that is exactly how I felt in that moment.

Then the air split open, and the formations of Blackshirts in front of us pulled apart, leaving a narrow corridor. There, we saw a thin hooded figure in chains, bent down and trembling with terror as two Blackshirts dragged them forward. The prisoner was clothed in tattered rags, soaked in dark blood that was still running down their legs and left a trail of red on the concrete. We watched on in horror, recognizing one of our own being marched toward the pyre.

I looked to my comrades, left and right, looked for someone to take responsibility, someone to stop this madness to which I felt complicit, but all I saw there was resignation and fear.

Blackshirts surrounded us to our left and front, grey soldiers to our right, ready to extinguish any attempt at revolt in an instant. We had no weapons and no protection;

we had only the filthy rags on us. I saw many of my comrades looking away as if they did not want to accept what was about to happen before their very own eyes.

The General stepped forward and addressed the hooded prisoner, who now trembled on the ground before us all.

"You must die", he intoned in a low commanding voice.

He motioned to the Blackshirts, who hoisted our struggling comrade onto the stake, tying rope to each arm and leg. The prisoner struggled to cry out in despair, but was quickly and brutally silenced by a soldier's elbow to the throat.

The General narrowed his eyes at us.

"This is justice!" he screamed, the veins on his neck pulsing with rage, his chest heaving, the white tower of his emblem shining in the light.

"THIS IS JUSTICE!" he shouted again and again, his face red with strain, spittle flying from his mouth, his gaze sweeping across the audience, daring someone, anyone, to voice their disagreement.

Nobody did.

Satisfied, he took a step backward and gestured to the Blackshirts, his wild eyes never leaving the crowd. From behind their formations, they now brought two barrels that I recognized immediately. The yellow liquid began to hiss and sizzle against the kindling as they emptied it onto the pyre, and a caustic smell filled the air, making it hard to breathe.

I saw our hooded comrade writhing and convulsing against the ropes, tears streaming down my face now. This would be the final nail in the coffin of our existence. After this was done, there would be no recovery. *Not ever*. And when I looked through the crowds, through tears and toxic air, I saw that it was true.

Then, after an order from the General, one of the Blackshirts climbed onto the pyre and stood beside the prisoner. Slowly, the soldier removed the hood that covered the prisoner's face.

I should have seen it coming.

I should have known.

Beneath the Blackshirt's outstretched arm, beneath the firm hand gripping the hood, I saw a face I knew very well. I had dreamed of this face, had seen it whenever I closed my eyes.

It had all started with her.

The hope, the purpose, the longing for freedom — inadvertently, she had begun the dream. When that grey soldier had saved her, he had saved us all.

And then the dam finally broke.

12

The world became a blur and time twisted and stretched, as too many things happened all at once. There was the heavy stomping of boots, a piercing scream of rage, and the smell of smoke and acid in the air.

Like in a dream, I saw one of the grey soldiers to our right hurl a flask filled with bright yellow liquid high into the air. There was a handkerchief sticking out of its opening, one end of it burning in a greenish flame. Broad shoulders, dark skin, and a bald head appeared out of the soldier's uniform and my heart lurched when I saw that the hand that had launched the vessel was adorned with a tattoo of a black hammer.

The burning flask hit the Blackshirts' screaming general and a moment later there appeared countless more of them, high in the air, cast from the ranks of the grey soldiers. A rain of fire landed among the Blackshirts, who scattered in surprise like ants exposed to sunlight.

The grey soldiers lifted their rifles as if to fire at us, the workers, but instead directed their shots at the panicked formations of Blackshirts, who responded with their heavy machine guns. In an instant, utter chaos ensued as we all ran for cover, dodging bullets, acid, and fire along the way.

As I scrambled away from the madness, I thought I could still make out the General's dying shrieks from behind me, and when I turned, I saw his face melting and twisting in agony.

And amidst all this turmoil, our comrade on the pyre stood tall, sentenced to death, her hands and feet still bound to the stake that had been intended for her execution — a stake that never burned. Thick smoke filled the air, making it difficult for me to see from my cover behind a pile of rubble, but I could have sworn she was smiling or laughing. Had she lost her mind? What kind of madness could allow her to remain so placid while death rained all around?

I saw the tattooed soldier crouching up to her, saw him climb the pyre with bullets raining down on him, until he stood by her side. With swift and determined movements, he untied her ropes and threw her down on the side of the pyre that was facing away from the Blackshirts. All the while, she kept on laughing like a maniac.

At first, I had been uncertain whether these grey soldiers, these former enemies of us, these cruel instruments of control and subjugation, were now our allies or not. Whether the tattooed soldier came to save our comrade or merely finish what the Blackshirts had started. But then, when I saw them fighting and dying in the hundreds, when I saw the blood and the injuries and the pain, bullets all around, I realized that we could trust them.

The other side of the same coin.

The same struggles. The same misery.

Now we were one. United against the tyranny of the Tower. I never thought this moment would arrive, but here we were. *The revolution had begun.*

With the woman pulled behind the safety of a stack of

bricks and two comrades tending to her wounds, the soldier with the black tattoo looked around, surveying the area with a cool, confident gaze. Then, when he saw me cowering behind the rubble, his eyes lit up and he motioned for me to come closer. There was no doubt whether I would answer his call.

Carefully I moved behind the front lines, while his grey brothers and sisters in arms pressed ahead, following the disarrayed Blackshirts to the far end of the cleared space. Many of them were already among the shadows of the machines, and I realized that this could turn into a long, drawn-out battle with no predictable outcome. And there would soon be many more Blackshirts spewing out from the Tower.

Once I arrived at his side, the tattooed soldier led me to an abandoned area of the Factory, away from the battlefield. There we found a series of identical warehouses made of red brick, each with a corrugated iron roof. They were built close together, packed like books on a crowded bookshelf, and, from the looks of it, the glass in their rectangular windows had been smashed an eternity ago.

He opened the gate to one of them, and I saw that it was filled with old, almost rotten, wooden crates.

"We have no weapons to give you," he said, his deep voice taking me by surprise. He picked up a crate from behind him and pried it open with his powerful hands. "But we have these."

I peered inside and saw that the crate was filled with hundreds of hammers. They were short and stubby, with pitted worn heads and wooden handles stained with the years. The metal was rusty and dull; the paint had chipped away. Some were bent and twisted from excessive use, while others were still relatively sharp but in desperate need of repair. Still, they looked marvelous to me.

He took one of them and held it out to me. It was remarkably heavy and felt oddly reassuring in my hand. I looked up into his weary eyes as he spoke:

"A hammer to break your shackles — if you want."

With a sad smile on his lips, he held out his hand.

"Trust me..."

He hesitated for a moment.

"Comrade."

I looked into his eyes and considered the briefest of moments. Then I shook his hand, and the union was formed.

I had made that decision a long time ago, I realized; when this soldier had risked everything to spare a woman he did not even know, a worker. There had been no reason for him to do so, and yet he did. And then, when he saved her again, from the fire and the flames, he started a war. She and him; they were the catalyst we had all been waiting for.

I felt myself coming back from the dead, from the darkness to which they had banished me. For the first time, I felt powerful.

"Let's get to work," he said.

We picked up the crates and moved them outside, where soldiers in grey began handing them out. Workers who had been waiting their entire lives for this very moment ran toward us and took the rusty hammers with tears in their eyes. They realized what was happening as soon as they saw me standing beside the tattooed soldier, a hammer in my hand.

"Why me?" I finally asked him.

He thought for a moment.

"Because you have seen me that day and because you know. You have been under the Tower and you came back.

You returned to work. You have nothing to lose and you will do everything. This is what it takes."

He gazed off into the distance. "I saw you when you were born, you know. I was there. You could not accept the darkness as easily as the others. You struggled, and you suffered. They had to keep you alive and then break you. To show that it was possible; to show that no one could escape, not even in thought, and to make an example. Still, here you are."

I nodded, thinking about his words and watching as more and more comrades appeared from all corners of the Factory. Watching as they cradled their hammers and looked at each other in wonder.

"Why did you do it?" I asked. "The woman?"

Momentarily, I saw him glance at the Tower and I could not tell whether it was with hatred or with longing. And I remember feeling an icy shiver at that.

"I had to," he answered. And then he disappeared, returning to the battlefield, barking orders at his greys along the way, while the sound of distant gunfire filled the air.

I had no time to think about him. The revolution that had only been a distant, impossible dream had suddenly turned into reality. And I knew I had to say something now. Knew I had to take responsibility. They were all looking at me, waiting for someone to ignite the spark.

"Comrades!"

It came as a whimper, entirely unsuitable to the moment. So I tried again, and I shouted with everything I had:

"COMRADES!"

This was met with a terrible roar, hammers raised to the sky. I felt a shiver run down my spine as my emotions ran rampant, my skin breaking out in goosebumps. I continued:

"These are the first words I speak to you, and they might be the last. I have not much to say."

I looked into their hopeful faces full of life and fire now. They embraced my words, even the grey soldiers still dealing out hammers, not because I had any sort of authority but because they had seen me at my lowest and they had seen me return. For whatever reason, I had witnessed both the soldier's actions and the gruesome death of the suit. I had been under the Tower, for how long I do not know, and I had returned an empty husk. And here I was again, not special, not stronger than the others, just always in the right places at the right times.

I thought about what to say next and then decided to just speak the truth. I screamed it at the top of my lungs, my body trembling both with rage and deep sorrow for those who had not made it so far. For the fallen who had spent their lives in darkness and without perspective, toiling for the benefit of others. I drew strength from the hammer in my hand and lifted it to join the others.

"WE HAVE NOTHING TO LOSE BUT OUR CHAINS!"

I was met with another terrible roar, and for a moment I thought I saw the Tower swaying. Hands reached up to the heavens, ready to take what was ours from the very beginning.

"NO ONE IS FREE — *NOT A SINGLE ONE OF US* — UNTIL WE ARE ALL FREE!"

The warehouses shook from the thunderous response; rats scattered into their holes; the air smelled of blood and ashes. The threshold had been passed and the masses, both rags and uniforms, had become ungovernable. There was no turning back now, no return to the status quo, and I started sobbing with relief.

The Factory

And amidst the crowd, I saw the woman with the short hair.

Barely able to stand, supported by those around her, she held her hammer up to the sky, a smile on her face and fire in her eyes. This woman who was alive because of a soldier; who had killed a suit, an untouchable, in the most gruesome way; who had been tortured for who knows how long; who had been ready to burn and then was saved again. She was the strongest of us all.

I watched as they all lifted their hammers, again and again, thousands upon thousands, a wave of iron. I gazed at the Tower as we let out a cry for freedom that shook the Factory and could be heard all the way to its golden crown. Soon, it would melt.

"Let's kill Blackshirts."

13

The war raged on for days and weeks, and the scars it left were apparent all around us.

The Factory was scorched and scarred, pocked with craters and littered with the twisted remains of machines and bodies; the air was still thick with the acrid smell of smoke, blood, and burning rubble; and the constant sound of explosions and gunfire filled the air.

Wounded and dying lay everywhere, their cries of pain and desperation adding to the chaos and confusion. Fresh and rotting corpses alike lay discarded in the streets, half-eaten by the rats, their blank, staring eyes a testament to what happened.

The mental toll of war was just as devastating as the physical one. Many of us struggled with the weight of our actions, plagued by nightmares and flashbacks of the horrors we had witnessed and inflicted ourselves. The trauma of war left deep wounds that would last a lifetime and beyond. There would be no healing from that, I realized.

And then, when we could almost go on no more, the soldier with the black tattoo led us into one last desperate attack, throwing everything we had left into it, and we drove the Blackshirts back to the Tower, where they barricaded themselves.

There had been so much fighting, rage, and suffering that when their retreat, swift and organized, happened, we were too numb for both celebration and mourning. We had achieved a great victory — but at what cost?

We walked around the Factory in a daze of shock and disbelief, blood dripping from our red rags and hammers, the grey soldiers' rifles still hot to the touch. The ground was soaked, bodies of men and women, workers, soldiers, Blackshirts, and suits alike strewn across. Our hearts were heavy with grief as we embraced and watched our comrades take their last breaths and listened to their final words. So much talk now; touches, emotion, after being denied all of it for as long as we could think.

Eventually, we regrouped and mustered our strength to plan our next move. We had successfully pushed the Blackshirts out of the Factory, but now we had to take on the Tower itself so that they could not return. *Not ever.*

To keep our defenses from being breached by surprise, we set up positions with rotating shifts right beneath the Tower. There, we lit bonfires in remembrance of those who had given their lives for the cause. We sang loud and heavy songs of freedom and we kept vigil. Watching the fires, embracing each other, we began talking and exchanging our stories.

We gave ourselves names. My comrades called me Pascal now. A suit — Ren, she named herself — had suggested the name as a joke and it had stuck. She had seen it written in many of the machines' manuals and thought it suited me. From what I gathered, it had something to do with the amount of pressure that could be applied until something had to give. The woman with the short hair we called Mars, and the soldier with the black tattoo was now known as

Hammer. He refused to choose a different name for himself, so we just stuck with calling him what he wanted to be. He wore it with pride.

Ren had been among the highest-ranking suits in the Factory. While most of them fled to the Tower as soon as the fighting started, and many others fell fighting alongside the Blackshirts, she and some of her assistants had ultimately joined our ranks.

There had been a lot of hesitation, fear, and heated debate about whether to accept their surrender instead of just killing them where they stood — their twisted long shapes and contorted faces, barely recognizable as human, had not helped their cause, and we all remembered, of course, what they had done to us.

Ultimately, cooler heads prevailed, and their surrender, and, in time, cooperation had been accepted. They were not all the same, we learned. Some of them had retained their humanity, clung unto it for all that time. Once they were freed, they became individuals again, able to make their own decisions — just like the grey soldiers.

At a certain point in the war, we had been forced against a wall; forced to decide who and what we wanted to be. What we wanted our revolution to mean and how it would be remembered. We decided then that, while for the moment, the violence was necessary and could not be avoided, we would not allow ourselves to turn into bloodthirsty monsters. We would not allow ourselves to become Blackshirts of another shade.

Not all of us were happy with that decision, however — especially some of the grey soldiers, who had now mostly become indistinguishable from us, but some of which still clung unto violence and cruelty as a means in itself.

Yes, the terrible violence. The one we saw and inflicted. It would be something we had to live with. Hopefully, those who come after will remember it for what it was: the only choice they gave us, the only thing they understood.

Since then, Ren and the other suits have proven themselves over and over, providing vital information on the enemies' weaknesses, operations, and the Factory itself. She and her assistants now typed away on their shiny rectangles, sitting among us at the campfires, telling tales of old. Of course, we never let them out of our sight. Not yet. For our protection and their own.

The Blackshirts were another story altogether. There was no redemption to be found among them. Even those we would allow to surrender kept on fighting like mindless machines of madness, programmed to do one thing and one thing only. On countless occasions, they proved their horrendous cruelty and inhumanity, never even hesitating, never even considering other paths.

They had to be defeated by hammer and rifle. There was no other way; not for them.

Oh, the violence, the horrible violence.

Did we do the right thing?

When I looked at the piles of bodies, the fat rats, their stomachs bulging from all the blood and the meat, I sometimes doubted. They had left us no choice. Why had they left us no choice? So much violence; I felt nauseous.

But when I thought about these things, and when I spoke with the others, we all agreed. *There was no choice*. There was nothing else but lifting those old rusty hammers, again and again and again, until there was freedom.

The violence we committed, the things we did. Ours was the revolution and the war, but the new world would be for the ones who come after.

The more I thought about this, the more I became convinced that there was no salvation waiting for us, no light at the end of the far too long, pitch-black tunnel. We were the middle children of history, destined to mine that tunnel to a better place, yet doomed to never live that life we longed for.

There was danger in that. We were not some band of benevolent, kindhearted saints. We were human, and not all of us would be willing to sacrifice and pass on. The more I thought about this, the more I realized that the actual war would be fought once the Tower was no more. When we would be left with the question *What now?;* when we would be left with a world to build.

The real war.

We would have to be careful.

Sometimes, when I looked at Mars, that woman who had been through more pain and suffering than most of us, her anger and rage obvious and never subsiding, and Hammer, that madman of a soldier, the two of them lovers now, I grew afraid.

How would they fit into the new world when all they had ever known was cruelty and violence? How would any of us fit when all we had ever known was misery and darkness? How could people who had never known love and friendship, kindness and companionship, community, justice, equality and self-determination build a world based upon these principles?

The more and more I thought about these things, the more I became convinced that our fiercest battle was yet to be fought.

Mars. A suit explained to us what her name meant, and

how could there be any name more fitting? After the pyre, she became one of our fiercest warriors. But she was cruel, and she had done things — things I would rather not think about.

Blackshirts, who already lay dying, kept alive because she had not been done yet. No one had stopped her, because she had earned that right. More than any of us, she did. But those things she had done... How can one come back from that? What would become of her, once there was no one left to bring her hammer down on? That hammer, so red with blood.

So we sat among the bonfires, and we talked, and we shared, and we thought of the Tower, always right in front of us. This monument of decadence with its gem-adorned ornaments and the terrible crown of gold. It had stopped growing, at least. Now it just stood there, biding its time, waiting. An endless needle among all the ruins and the rats.

Hammer told us of his betrayal and how he had sought allies among his soldiers. He told us of the purges and the thousands who were executed by the Blackshirts when they began suspecting. He told us how the grey soldiers were trained and drilled to follow orders unquestionably and unhesitatingly, chosen by hand from the ranks of the workers to oversee their own; how he had sown seeds of doubt and dreams of freedom among them; and, ultimately, how he had used their loyalty to him to pit them against the Blackshirts.

And I thought about those things as well, because who would those soldiers follow when it came down to it? Their commander or the cause?

Most of them had become comrades, brothers and sisters in arms, fighting side by side with us, and I was sure that they would never betray us. But what about those who hadn't? Those who rejoiced and thrived in the free expression of violence, now that the constraints were off?

The fires crackled, and we talked some more about all those things that needed to be done. And we fought, and we quarreled among ourselves, for we were only human. For the first time, we imagined that new world we would build. And all the time I feared for this future. I would not voice those fears, for they were better left for after. Still, the Tower and its golden crown stood right in front of us. Still, we lived in darkness in an endless factory among the machines and the rats.

Our fight was not done yet. There would be time to talk about the after, but that time had not arrived yet.

We were not done! *We had achieved nothing.*

Weeks, months passed in this uncertainty, with both sides waiting for the other to make their next move. We had the Tower surrounded and under siege; they could not escape, and at some point, they would have to run out of the resources we used to produce for them. The Tower could not abide stagnation, it had to grow or it would collapse all on its own. We waited for them to fight back, to surrender, to collapse, and then... who knows?

But, alas, one day, as we gathered among the campfires, telling stories of old, Ren stood up tall, her impossibly long arms gripping her shiny rectangle. Loudly, she proclaimed:

"They sent a message. They want to talk!"

And then, when I gazed into Hammer's eyes and looked at some of the soldiers next to him, illuminated by the flickering flames, my fears gave way to an overwhelming sense of dread and I knew what needed to be done.

14

They chose Mars, Hammer, and me to represent the revolution, and I could not help but feel that they granted the three of us too much authority. They made us into their leaders; they delegated responsibility, and there was danger in that. It made us all vulnerable.

Mars and Hammer accepted their roles immediately, and I worried about that, too. In the end, I had no choice but to comply, and so I walked to the Tower right alongside them, followed by two dozen of Hammer's most loyal soldiers.

I gripped my hammer; it felt heavier than ever. I looked around, and I saw the ruins of the Factory, the empty alleys, the silent machines, and the smoke of distant fires. We had done this, all of us, together. We had come this far. But what would it all be for?

We kept walking until we reached the entrance to the Tower. I took a deep breath, and we waited. Then, after a short while, the impenetrable gates opened with a deep groan. We stepped inside the Tower for the first time, and it felt like we had stepped into a different world.

We stood there in stunned silence, our eyes wide with disbelief. We had come expecting to find a merciless, black-shirted general; instead, we found ourselves in the presence of what appeared to be gods.

Before us, on colossal golden thrones, sat three stunning, gracious figures, two men and one woman. They were adorned in luxurious garments and elegant woolen capes, the likes of which I had never seen before. Each of them wore a unique crown and had a regal, otherworldly beauty about their pale white features.

Never had I felt such inferiority as in this moment. Who were we to question these angelic creatures? Who were we to doubt their wisdom? I looked down at my blood-stained rags, my bare broken feet, the hammer in my hands, and could not help but feel ashamed.

As I took in the grandeur of the hall, trying to avert my gaze from those gods, my eyes were drawn to the perfectly polished white marble walls. Hanging on these walls were massive portraits, each showing a different deity with a countenance as pale as the marble that surrounded them. The frames of these portraits were adorned with elaborate wood carvings, adding an extra layer of opulence to the already grandiose scene. Unseeable eyes seemed to watch us from everywhere, observing with unrivaled intelligence.

Then, the god sitting in the middle stood up from his throne, standing tall and proud, and with a slight gesture of his feeble, uncalloused hands motioned for us to approach him. He spoke with a deep voice that seemed to match his majestic appearance and made me grip my hammer even tighter. I barely dared to look up at this nobility.

"We have called on you to discuss matters regarding your so-called revolution," he said.

And then he promised us everything.

We would live in the highest reaches of the Tower, he said, and our every need would be taken care of. We would have food, clothing, riches, and comfort beyond our imaginations. The three of us would be free from the tyranny of them, our oppressors, free to do whatever we desired, and we would never again have to take up hammer, wrench, or rifle.

Even our comrades outside — workers, soldiers, and suits — he did not forget. He promised that they, too, would live better lives. That we would not have to worry about them. They would have to return to work, of course, so that the Tower could keep on growing, but they would be granted better clothes, food, from time to time, and even rest. The rats would be dealt with, and they would be allowed to bury their dead now. They would recall the Blackshirts. Workers, soldiers, and suits would live in better conditions than they ever did before.

In exchange for this, all we would have to do was lay down our weapons, surrender, and accept that even when we'd live among them, we would never be like them. That always would they be our masters and we their servants; gods and insects. That never again would we attempt to change what cannot be changed; the natural order of things that would be maintained and guarded forever. Generation after generation, born and buried, would contribute to the glory of the Tower.

"Do you not see that the Tower's growth benefits us all?" he asked. "Workers must toil, suits must manage, soldiers must discipline, and we must rule so that we all may progress. Ultimately, we will reach the heavens. All together, we will rise above."

"Do you not desire prosperity and abundance for all your people?", he inquired with a warm smile on his face, spreading his arms and offering everything.

The two gods to his sides beamed down upon us, urging

us to take this offer, for it would never be extended again. And while I could not deny the allure of their proposal and the story of collective progress they spun, I could not bring myself to accept it. I stood there, motionless, with my heart pounding in my chest and my eyes filling up with tears.

It was all lies, all of it. Wasn't it?

There would be no prosperity for all; there could not be as long as the Tower stood and these false gods ruled.

It was nothing but an instrument of control, the Tower, I saw. Built to sustain the status quo forever. These gods writhing in wealth and comfort, walking their grand halls, while we would keep building their monuments of vain, under the false hope that we'd someday reach the heavens. And if not in this world, then in the afterlife.

Lies! All of it!

We had fought long and hard, had spilled gallons of blood to come so far. The bodies of our comrades decorated the streets and filled the rats. There was no way we would just let it all slip from our fingers. And for what? For greed?

My vision swam around the hall, swaying and taking it all in, until my gaze rested on Mars. I saw the hatred and rage burning in her eyes, still, and a wave of relief washed over me. Never would she accept these terms; never would she live in the Tower. But then my eyes found Hammer's face and my heart lurched. His features were solemn and stern as he spoke with a deep rumble in his chest.

"We need more," he said; a command that resonated with finality. His bald head glimmered like a crystal pearl. "Give us more and we will talk."

I went to him then, on unsteady legs, my arms gripping his, embracing my brother, my comrade, pleading.

"Please..." I stammered, my voice barely a whisper.

But when I looked into his eyes, I realized it was a lost cause. He would not be deterred.

As I stood there, collapsed in his arms and facing the impossible, I felt a sense of deep calm wash over me. I had tried to ignore that constant nagging feeling in the back of my mind, the one that told me this moment was inevitable. But now, as I stared at the seemingly insurmountable challenge, I knew there was no avoiding it any longer. I had to take control, no matter how much I feared it. Just this once. *It needed to be done.*

My heart pounded in my chest as I took a deep breath and stepped away from the grey soldier I had called comrade. It was he who had insisted on meeting, even though we had the Tower surrounded and it seemed only a matter of time before it collapsed. It was he who had insisted on listening to what they had to say. And now I knew why.

From a fold within my filthy blood-drenched rags, secured there with tape, I quickly withdrew the small shiny rectangle Ren had given me. I went to Mars and took her hands in mine. Her eyes seemed full of regret and sorrow for what might have been. For the future we never got to experience. This woman, who had only lived in hell.

"Forgive me," I said, as I saw the faces of the gods contort and twist with understanding.

They were too late.

I gave the signal, and the world around us disintegrated.

The foundations of reality shook as destruction descended upon this mortal realm. Mars' hands were trembling in mine, but I held on tight, trying to anchor us both to something stable. It was as if the universe was coming apart at the seams, and there was nothing we could do to stop it.

The ceilings and walls of the hall buckled and groaned, and then, with a thunderous explosion of dust and light, they caved in. The deafening sound obliterated all other thought, and I felt her embracing me as tightly as she could.

I saw Hammer buried beneath a boulder; I saw his soldiers attempting to flee, but there was no escape now; I saw the gods' useless fury; and I saw the Tower collapse.

With a final, desperate look into each other's eyes, we braced ourselves for the end. Finally, our endless struggle would cease.

In these last moments, I thought I smelled grass and flowers. Was there peace to be found on the other side?

15

Workers, soldiers, and suits watched from a distance as the barrels erupted from within the depths of the Tower.

After the deafening explosion and the blinding light, there came a moment of tense silence, as if the world was holding its breath, and then the Tower, that monument to human decadence and greed, finally began to crumble.

It was a slow, agonizing process at first, as the foundations of the structures shook and cracked, ceilings and walls submitting to the terrible forces. They watched on in horror and awe as the upper levels of the Tower, almost too high to make out, started to lean and sway, struggling to stay upright. Then, when the golden crown began melting, they fled in a panic, trying to escape the falling rubble.

Some of them were caught in the chaos, crushed under the weight of the falling debris, buried beneath molten gold and white marble. The screams of the injured and dying echoed through the air, adding to the cacophony of destruction. The air was thick with smoke and dust, making it difficult to see or breathe, and the smell of acid filled the Factory.

The survivors huddled together then, hiding beneath the machines with their bodies closely pressed to the hard, cold concrete floor, safe from the deadly rain of rubble. There, they lay as their world disintegrated. And then, after minutes that stretched like hours, through the smoke and the dust, one of them pointed out a crack in the heavens.

Jagged gaping tears appeared in the blackness, spreading all across the visible sky and to the horizon in all directions. Through these holes in reality, light started pouring into their world, illuminating the Factory, scattering the rats, brighter than anything they had ever seen before.

The sun shone down on them like the embrace of a long-lost but never quite forgotten friend, and they felt its warmth radiate through their bodies. The rays danced over their faces, those dirty, blood-stained features sticking out from beneath the machines, blinding them in one moment and then plunging them into cool shadow in the next.

And when they looked at each other, all they saw was laughter. They rejoiced and shouted in the safety beneath the machines as the sky was coming down on them; rubble, concrete, steel, marble, glass, and all, raining down from distant heights.

They embraced each other as the smoke and the dust fought an ultimately losing battle against the piercing light, and they cried in sorrow for those that had bravely gone into the Tower and sacrificed it all. Worker, soldier, or suit, it did not matter now. In the dust and the dirt, they all looked the same.

The rain lasted for hours, days, weeks; time was hard to tell. And then, when it ceased, the survivors, comrades all, brothers and sisters, emerged from beneath the machines they had worked their entire lives. They cleared the rubble and dust from each other and then they gathered the dead, using hands and tools to recover as many as they could.

The Factory

When they could find no more, they started walking.

Together, they wandered to the ends of the collapsed factory, many times across the horizon, carrying the dead. There they saw the edges and walls that were gone, all collapsed, revealing the endless freedom beyond. With the last of their strength, they climbed over the rubble and the broken machines, out of breath and drenched in sweat. They helped each other and still they carried the dead.

And then the survivors emerged from the depths of the Factory, stepping over the border and onto the grass, greeted by a vista of magnificent beauty.

The fields that spread out before them were a riot of color, with long, lush grasses and wildflowers in bloom. The air was sweet with the scent of fresh growth, and the sun, so long absent from their lives, warmed their faces. Many of them collapsed in joy, just lying there in the grass, their senses overwhelmed, unable to comprehend it all.

They laid down their rifles, their hammers and their wrenches, their shiny rectangles, and they left them in the Factory. The next time they would wield a tool, it would be of their own volition.

And after they had buried their dead and spoken a few words, they made their way to the river, a ribbon of shimmering silver that wound its way through the fields.

They followed its course, drawn by the soothing sound of its flow and the promise of refreshment. And as they approached the water's edge, they were struck by the beauty of the scene before them. The river was a living, breathing thing, its surface rippled by the gentle currents that flowed beneath. The sunlight danced upon the waters, casting a golden glow on the trees and grasses that lined its banks.

The survivors knelt by the water's edge and drank

deeply of the cool, clear liquid. It flowed through them like a tonic, washing away the sorrow and pain that had weighed upon their hearts. They basked in the momentary splendor, letting the peace of the river wash over them. And as they sat by its sides, they started talking about their new lives. They had no gods now, no masters, and no leaders; no one to tell them what to do. They were free; free after all, and they would make their own mistakes. And they would rejoice in them, for they were theirs to make.

When they were rested, they started walking, hand in hand, to the top of the hill, taking in the majesty of the surrounding universe.

There, they stood in awe, marveling at the birds that soared overhead, blackbirds and starlings, their wings outstretched as they rode the currents of the air. The birds sang out, their voices a chorus of life and hope, and the survivors responded with laughter and trembling cries of delight.

The world welcomed them back, the animals, the plants, the trees, and everything alive, all part of the same thing; accepting them for what they were, forgiving, despite everything they had done. And as the survivors stood there, a gust of wind, full of force and energy, swept over them. It captured them in its embrace, sending cold shivers down their spines and filling their bodies with fire.

They knew in that moment that they had returned home.

That this is where they belong.

The Story Continues

Echoes of Tyranny: Freedom Lost

Book 2 of the Factory Saga

What can I tell you of freedom that you do not feel yourself? What can I tell you of the people of the valley that you would not recognize in those around you?

There is community and kindness, and there is anger and conflict too, for we are only human. The first after the Factory, and perhaps the last. I wish it were different, yet I feel it, know it in my heart, that nothing can last forever. This planet was not made for our kind. It's all wilting away, dust in our hands, and we are strangers.

There is a storm on the horizon and a darker one in our midst. Did we escape the Factory? Are we the heirs of the revolution or are we doomed, destined to fight this war over and over, until there is nothing?

More information on:
antoniomelonio.substack.com

About the Author

Antonio Melonio is an anarcho-communist writer, author, and content creator from the Balkans. Apart from writing novels and short stories, he is also the creator of *Beneath the Pavement*, in which he publishes essays and articles in addition to his fictional works.

Antonio Melonio had the great 'luck' of being born in the banana-nation of Bosnia and Herzegovina. A needless war, in which thousands died and that left everyone worse off than before, forced his parents to move to the even-more-banana-nation of Austria, where he grew up and learned of 'Western values.' He holds a master's degree in business economics (he was young and astoundingly stupid), and another useless bachelor's degree in teacher education. His day job, right now (it changes on a monthly basis), is teaching high school mathematics and physics to unwilling students with an attention span similar to his.

Antonio Melonio is the author of *The Factory: Revolution's Call, Echoes of Tyranny: Freedom Lost, The Eagle's Shadow: Winter Reign, Cyan Waters: A Story From the Poolrooms*, and dozens of essays and articles.

Manufactured by Amazon.ca
Bolton, ON